Birdwoman Interview

Written by Jill Eggleton
Illustrated by Philip Webb

Rigby

Birdwoman Interview

Interview by Tim Shelley

Henrietta Higgins is the Birdwoman of Brinwick. She is called the Birdwoman because birds follow her. She has made her home into a Bird Hospital where she takes care of sick and hurt birds.

How do the birds get to your Bird Hospital?

I go out and save sick and hurt birds. I have saved baby birds that have fallen out of their nests. Once I saved a bird from a high cliff. I had to swing down on a rope from a helicopter. One day I saved a bird that was caught in some shorts on a clothesline. It was tangled up in the legs. I had to untangle the shorts to free it.

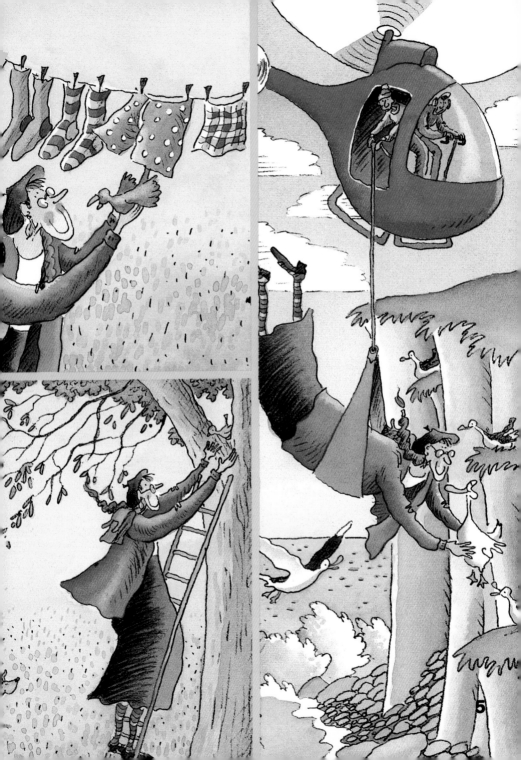

5

Where do you keep the birds?

The sick birds can't fly. I keep them
in my house. My house has bird beds
everywhere. It looks like a hospital.
When the birds start to get better,
I put them into a bedcage.

What is a bedcage?

A bedcage is just a word that I made up. It is a room for birds who are getting better. My house has four bedrooms. I made the bedrooms into four big bedcages.

8

What is a bedcage like inside?

Bedcages are like a garden. I didn't want the birds to feel they were in a cage. Each bedcage has a tree and plants in pots. The roof has a glass window so the birds can see the sky.

11

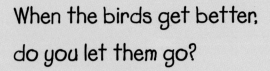

When the birds get better, do you let them go?

Yes. I take them outside and watch them fly away. Sometimes they don't want to fly away at all. Sometimes they stay. That is why I have hundreds of birds in my garden.

13

Grumpy people say the birds leave
droppings everywhere. They say the
birds make too much noise. They do
make a lot of noise in the morning.
I have to wear earmuffs to bed.

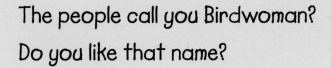

The people call you Birdwoman?
Do you like that name?

Yes, I do. I am a birdwoman. The birds follow me everywhere. They sit on my shoulders when I walk. They follow my car. When they follow my car, it is not very safe. It is good when drivers let me go past them. I don't need a siren like a police officer. I am happy to be a birdwoman.

Interviews

Interviews inform people about the interesting events, thoughts, and feelings of the person being interviewed. Interviews can be written in question-and-answer formats.

I ask the questions. I'm the interviewer.

I answer the questions. I'm the interviewee.

Writing an Interview

Step One Introduce the interviewee.
Henrietta Higgins is the Birdwoman of Brinwick.

Step Two Tell the audience why the interviewee is an interesting person.
She is called the Birdwoman because birds follow her. She has made her home into a Bird Hospital.

Step Three Ask questions that will find out unusual and interesting information about the interviewee's life, thoughts, and feelings.

I go out and save sick and hurt birds.

I didn't want birds to feel they were in a cage.

I am happy to be a birdwoman.

Guide Notes

Title: Birdwoman Interview

Stage: Fluency

Text Form: Interview

Approach: Guided Reading

Processes: Thinking Critically, Exploring Language, Processing Information

Written and Visual Focus: Interview, Speech Bubbles, Plan

THINKING CRITICALLY
(sample questions)
- What do you think is interesting about the birdwoman?
- Why do you think the birdwoman made her home into a bird hospital?
- Why do you think some birds don't want to fly away from the birdwoman's garden?
- If you were the person asking the questions, what else might you ask the birdwoman?

EXPLORING LANGUAGE

Terminology
Spread, author and illustrator credits, ISBN number

Vocabulary
Clarify: interview, tangled, untangled, earmuffs
Nouns: birds, hospital, helicopter, rope, garden
Verbs: swing, fly
Singular/plural: bird/birds, house/houses

Print Conventions
Apostrophe – contraction (didn't)

Phonological Patterns
Focus on short and long vowel **a** (s**a**ved, m**a**de, c**a**ge, h**a**s, th**a**t)
Discuss root words – fallen, getting
Look at suffix **y** (grump**y**)
Look at prefix **un** (**un**tangle)